To: Jack
Love From: Santa
Christmas 1993

To my parents Harry and Julia

VIKING
Published by the Penguin Group
Viking Penguin, a division of Penguin Books USA Inc.,
375 Hudson Street, New York, New York 10014, U.S.A.
Penguin Books Australia Ltd, Ringwood, Victoria, Australia
Penguin Books Canada Ltd, 2801 John Street, Markham, Ontario, Canada L3R 1B4
Penguin Books (N.Z.) Ltd, 182-190 Wairau Road, Auckland 10, New Zealand

First published in Great Britain by ABC 1990
First American Edition published in 1991

1   3   5   7   9   10   8   6   4   2

Copyright © Lucy Dickens, 1990
All rights reserved

Library of Congress catalog number: 90-50130
ISBN 0-670-83578-1

Printed and bound in Hong Kong by Imago Services (HK) Ltd.

Dirty

Henry

LUCY DICKENS

VIKING

Henry never looked neat.
Even when Lily brushed him,
he still looked wild and woolly.
As soon as Lily turned her
back, Henry ran off with his
friends and got dirty.

He jumped into muddy ponds,

played hide and seek at the farmer's,

searched the trash for tasty bones,

dug for rabbits in burrows,

and always rolled in the
blackberry patch at the bottom
of the garden before he came
in for supper.

One day, Lily and her mother
met him in the garden.

"You're not coming in until
Miss Pink has given you a
shampoo and haircut!" scolded
Lily's mother.

Lily dragged Henry to Miss Pink's.

Henry looked at Miss Pink.
Miss Pink looked at Henry.

"I do like a challenge!" she exclaimed
to Lily. "Come back in two hours."

She grabbed Henry and
plunged him into a sink
full of hot soapy water.

Just as Henry started to recover from the
shock, Miss Pink turned a cold shower over
his head.

At last, Henry was swept up
into a warm, dry towel and
rubbed all over.

He even opened his eyes again.
But there was worse to come.

Miss Pink whipped out
a large brush and started
pulling at the tangles and
knots in Henry's hair.

And when that was finished, she started
to cut his hair with a snip! snap! snip!
Henry watched his hair fall to the floor
in chunks.

Then she put what was left of his hair into
curlers and popped him under the hairdryer.
Henry closed his eyes once more.

When Henry dared to open
his eyes again, he blinked.
"There!" stated Miss Pink
with satisfaction. "Don't you
look nice!"

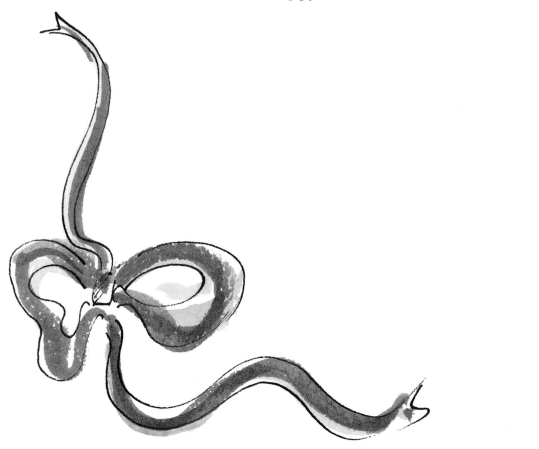

But when Lily arrived to take
him home, Henry wouldn't look
at her.

He slunk down the street.

He wouldn't come out from
under his favorite chair
for his supper.

But when no one was looking, Henry came
out and ran into the garden.

And that's where Lily found
him — in the blackberry patch,
rolling on his back.

"Oh, Henry!" she said as she
hugged him.

"I like you better when you're
happy and dirty!"